LADYBIRD BOOKS, INC.
Auburn, Maine 04210 U.S.A.
© LADYBIRD BOOKS LTD 1990
Loughborough, Leicestershire, England

Printed in England (3)

Night of the
Dinosaurs

By Joan Stimson
Illustrated by Maxie Chambliss

Ladybird Books

"I *wish* there still were dinosaurs," said Danny Duncan. He said it every day.

It had all started when Danny was a baby. His parents had taken him to a museum.

"Just look at this tyrannosaurus!" cried Mr. Duncan.

"Hey, check out this diplodocus!" exclaimed Mrs. Duncan.

Danny had been dinosaur-crazy ever since.

At an early age, Danny threw away his teddy bear—
and asked for a cuddly stegosaurus! As he grew up, he
filled his room with dinosaur books and posters. By the
time he went to school, Danny was a dinosaur expert.

At first Danny's teacher, Miss Fletcher, was pleased. "Why, Danny," she said, "you know more about dinosaurs than I do!"

But then she got impatient.

"Danny Duncan, there's nothing in your head but dinosaurs! Can't you think about *anything* else?"

Danny just shook his head. "I *wish* there still were dinosaurs," he sighed.

One day Danny's class went on a trip to the zoo.

The children rushed from one animal to the next—
all except Danny.

At the end of the trip, Nancy Newton made a special speech to thank the zookeeper. But halfway through the speech, there was a loud wail:

"I *wish* there still were dinosaurs!"

"Be *quiet*, Danny Duncan!" shouted Miss Fletcher.

Nancy was furious.

Mr. and Mrs. Duncan were going to a party that night. Danny was going to sleep over at Nancy Newton's house.

"Nancy's got a new tent," Danny's mother told him. "Maybe you'll be able to camp out in her back yard."

"Oh, boy!" said Danny.

When Danny got to Nancy's house, there was a note waiting for him. He opened it up. It said:

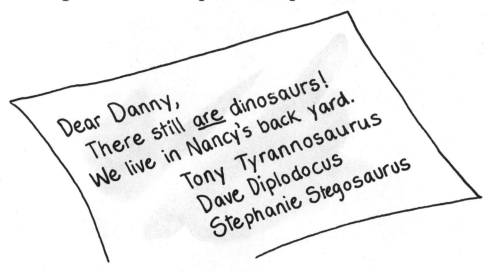

Dear Danny,
There still <u>are</u> dinosaurs!
We live in Nancy's back yard.
Tony Tyrannosaurus
Dave Diplodocus
Stephanie Stegosaurus

"Wow!" cried Danny. He put the note in his overnight bag. Then he and Nancy crawled into the tent.

"Let's turn on the light," Danny said. "I'll show you my new dinosaur book."

"Don't be ridiculous," said Nancy. "Tents don't have lights!"

"Oh," said Danny. He was beginning to feel a little nervous. He'd never slept in a tent before.

"Nightie-night," said Nancy. "Don't let the dinosaurs bite."

"What do you mean?" asked Danny, beginning to feel even more nervous.

But Nancy was already snoring.

Danny couldn't stop thinking about the note. He tried to remember if dinosaurs needed much sleep. His last thought before he dropped off was: "I *wish* there still were dinosaurs...*but not at night!*"

Danny tossed and turned. Dinosaurs filled his dreams. One looked like the zookeeper. One looked like Miss Fletcher. And one looked like Nancy's mother. They were all wearing party hats.

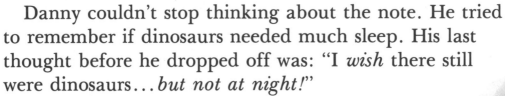

"We like going out at night!" they said.

Danny woke up in a panic. "Nancy!" he cried.

But Nancy had disappeared. Danny could just read the note on her pillow.

The moon went behind a cloud. An owl hooted.
Danny had never, ever been so scared.

Slowly, very slowly, Danny opened the tent flap. He peered into the darkness. And then he saw it—a terrible tyrannosaurus!

Danny gulped. He tried to forget that a tyrannosaurus had eight-inch teeth.

"T-T-Tony," he croaked, "have you got Nancy?"

There was no answer.

Then Danny looked closer — and saw that the tyrannosaurus was just a row of bushes.

"Phew," he said, and added bravely, "I *wish* there still were dinosaurs... *but not in Nancy's yard!*"

Suddenly something rustled. Danny turned and saw an enormous white shape looming in the moonlight. It was a dreadful diplodocus!

Danny shivered. He tried to forget that a diplodocus was about ninety feet long.

"D-D-Dave," he squeaked, "I'm looking for Nancy."

There was no reply.

Then Danny looked closer—and saw that the white shape was just clothes hanging on the line.

"Phew!" he said. He was very relieved. But not for long.

Strange noises came from behind the tent. Danny crept around to peek — and then he saw it! A spiky stegosaurus!

Danny jumped a mile.

"S-S-Stephanie," he squawked. He tried not to think about how sharp those spikes were. "Please give back Nancy."

"YOU'VE GOT IT!" cried a cheerful voice.

You could have knocked Danny down with a dandelion! The stegosaurus was only the Newtons' shed. Its spikes were the funny shingles on the roof. And Nancy was standing in the doorway!

"I wrote those notes," she said. "Were you scared?"

"Maybe a little," said Danny. He felt pretty silly.

"Serves you right for spoiling my speech," said Nancy. *She* felt pretty smart.

Danny and Nancy lay awake for a long time. Danny didn't feel like talking about dinosaurs, so Nancy told him about all the things he'd been missing. And just before they fell asleep, she recited her zoo speech—right to the end.

The next day at school, Miss Fletcher was still angry.

"Do you have anything to say today, Danny?" she asked.

Danny stood up. He took a deep breath.

"I *wish*..." he began, "I wish that I could go swimming and hiking and learn judo and ice skating and play baseball and soccer and get good grades. And most of all, I wish that next time we go to the zoo...that *I* could make the speech to the zookeeper."

"Good heavens!" said Miss Fletcher. "But what about dinosaurs?"

"Dinosaurs," declared Danny Duncan, "are a thing of the past—and *belong in museums!*"